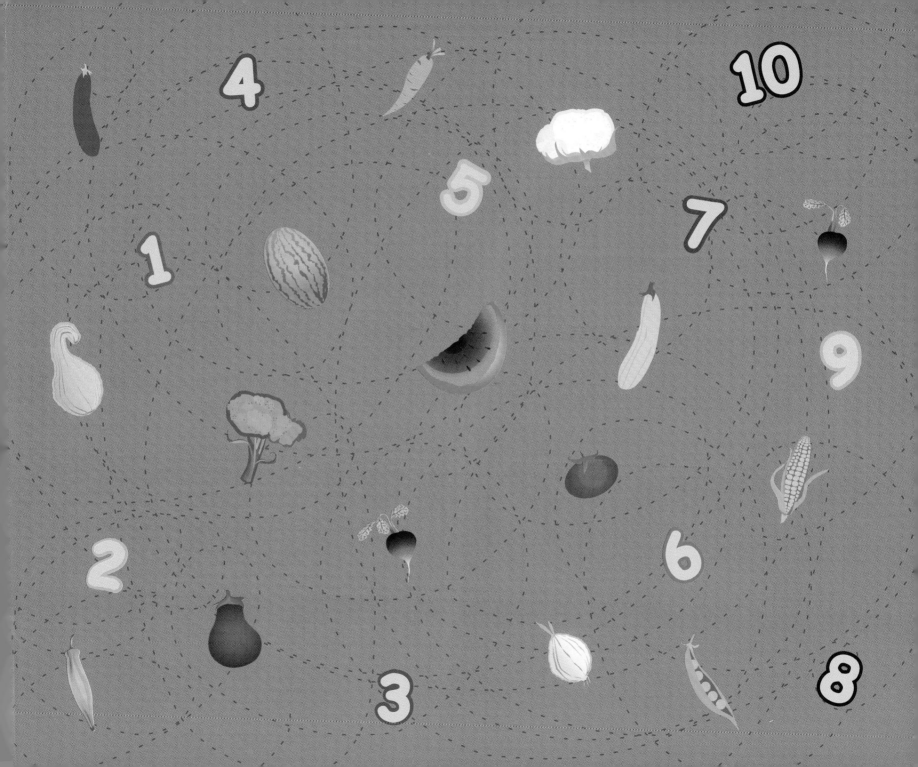

For Paula Witt
—B. M.

For Melanie Sampson
—M. S.

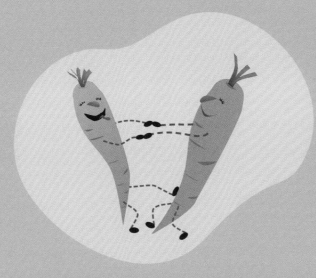

For Patrick and
my family
—H. C.

Henry Holt and Company, LLC, Publishers since 1866, 115 West 18th Street, New York, New York 10011

Henry Holt is a registered trademark of Henry Holt and Company, LLC
Text copyright © 2001 by Bill Martin Jr and Michael Sampson.
Illustrations copyright © 2001 by Heather Cahoon. All rights reserved.
Published in Canada by Fitzhenry & Whiteside Ltd., 195 Allstate Parkway, Markham, Ontario L3R 4T8.

Library of Congress Cataloging-in-Publication Data
Martin, Bill.
Rock it, sock it, number line / by Bill Martin, Jr and Michael Sampson; illustrations by Heather Cahoon.
Summary: Introduces the numbers one through ten as vegetables and numbers dance together at the
king's and queen's garden party before jumping into the soup to be eaten by a crowned boy and girl.
[1. Vegetables—Fiction. 2. Gardens—Fiction. 3. Dance—Fiction. 4. Counting. 5. Stories in rhyme.]
I. Sampson, Michael R. II. Cahoon, Heather, ill. III. Title.
PZ8.3.M3988Ro 2001 [E]—dc21 00-47134

ISBN 0-8050-6304-8 /First Edition—2001
The artist used Adobe® Illustrator to create the illustrations for this book. Designed by Martha Rago
Printed in the United States of America on acid-free paper. ∞
10 9 8 7 6 5 4 3 2 1

ROCK IT, SOCK IT, NUMBER LINE

BILL MARTIN JR
Michael Sampson

1 2 3

ILLUSTRATIONS BY **Heather Cahoon**

HENRY HOLT AND COMPANY   NEW YORK

On the castle side
of the garden green,
vegetables grow
for the king and queen.

The SUN IS HOT,
the day IS LONG,
and the veggies SING
their garden SONG.

AROUND THE GARDEN,
REGAL AND TALL,
TEN BRAVE GUARDS
AWAIT THE CALL.

"EVERYBODY DANCE,"
PROCLAIMS THE KING,
"FIND A PARTNER.
LET'S ALL SWING!"

ONE ROCKETS THROUGH THE SKY, AND PARACHUTES DOWN WITH A PUMPKIN PIE.

TWO FLIPS
INTO THE AIR,

LANDS ON THE BACK
OF A HUNGRY HARE.

THREE grabs
the okra plants,
and off they go
to the garden dance.

FOUR sees ONION,
SWINGS HER HIGH.
IN COMES LADYBUG,
and OFF THEY FLY.

FIVE buzzes in
on a bumblebee,
and circles
round the broccoli tree.

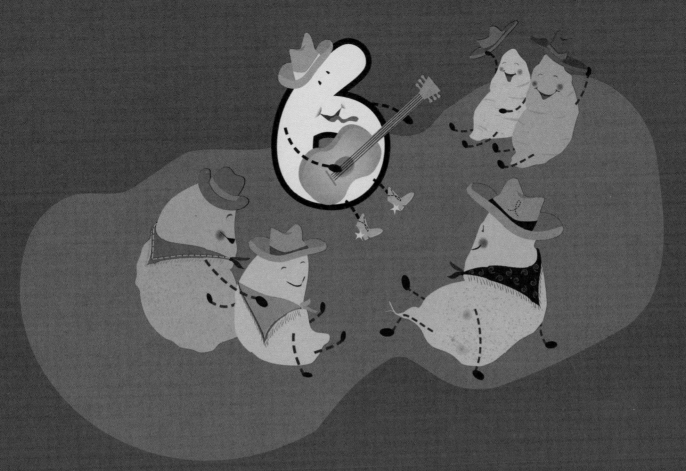

SIX arrives

with an old guitar,

tells the yams

he's a COUNTRY STAR!

SeveN sees TOMaTO
baSKING IN THE SUN,
TaKes HeR HaND,
aND OFF THEY RUN.

EIGHT comes dancing,
keeping time,
but trips and falls
on a melon vine.

NINE CALLS OUT,
"WAIT FOR ME!
I WANT TO BE IN
THE GARDEN SPREE!"

TeN YELLS OUT,
"WHAT GREAT FUN.
LET'S ROCK 'N' ROLL
TILL THE DAY IS DONE!"

NINE, EIGHT, SEVEN, and SIX

TWISTED IN

THE GARDEN MIX.

Five, FOUR,
THREE, and TWO,
dancing, prancing
number crew!

ONE bows proudly
TO THE KING.
EVERYBODY READY?
LET'S ALL SING . . .

"ROCK IT, SOCK IT,
NUMBER LINE!

NUMBERS AND VEGGIES—
PARTY TIME!"

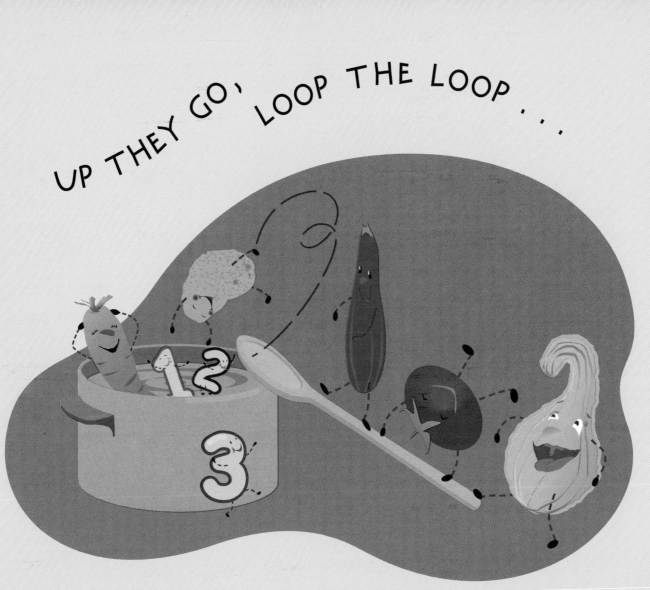